F
HAI   Haidle, Elizabeth

         Elmer the Grump

14.80

Maranatha Christian Academy

3800 S. Fairview Road

Santa Ana, CA 92704

ELMER
····· the ·····
GRUMP

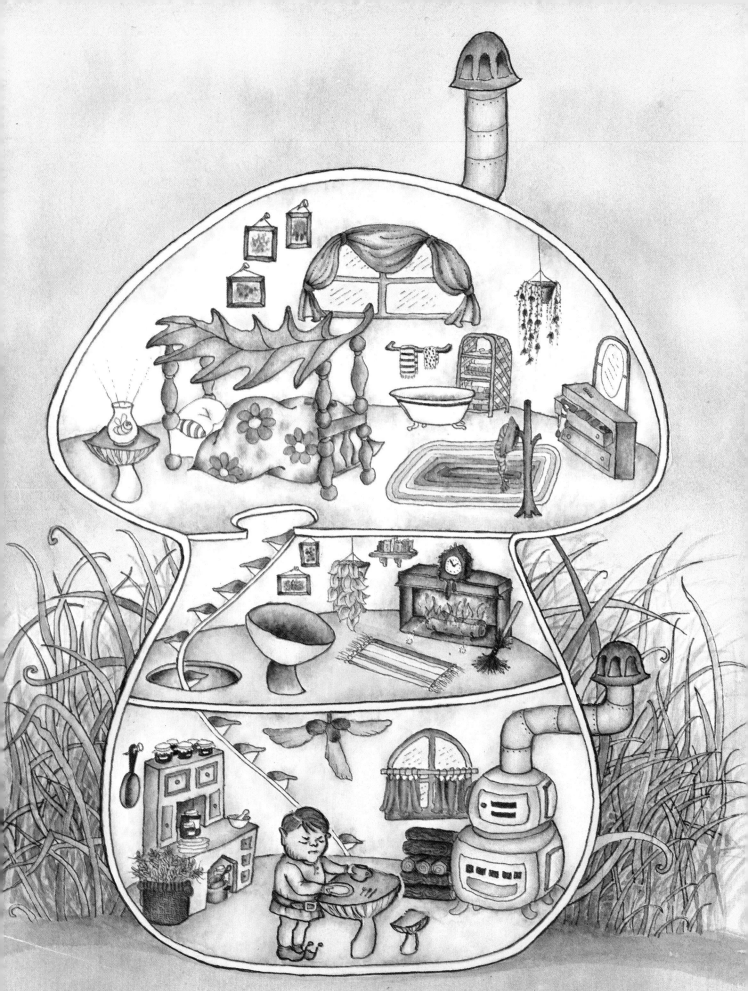

The house that Elmer builds.

ELMER the GRUMP

~ written & illustrated by ~

ELIZABETH HAIDLE

LANDMARK EDITIONS, INC.

P.O. Box 4469 • 1420 Kansas Avenue • Kansas City, Missouri 64127
(816) 241-4919

Dedicated to

my best friend, Heather;
my dear Oma;
and Grandpa and Grandma;
and most of all, to my family —
Dad, Mom, Jonathan and Paul.
This book would not have been possible
without their love and encouragement.

COPYRIGHT © 1989 BY ELIZABETH HAIDLE

International Standard Book Number: 0-933849-20-6 (LIB.BDG.)

Library of Congress Cataloging-in-Publication Data
Haidle, Elizabeth, 1974-
    Elmer the Grump.
    Summary: An unsociable, wood-carving elf changes his grumpy ways after
rescuing an injured snail.
    [1. Elves — Fiction.   2. Conduct of life — Fiction.
    3. Children's writings.]

I. Title.
PZ7.H1258El   1989   [E] — dc19   89-31872

Editorial Coordinator: Nancy R. Thatch
Creative Coordinator: David Melton

Printed in the United States of America

Landmark Editions, Inc.
P.O. Box 4469
1420 Kansas Avenue
Kansas City, Missouri 64127
(816) 241-4919

10083

ELMER THE GRUMP

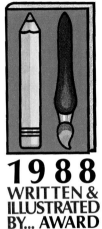

In our fast-paced society of quick foods and instant entertainment there are great misconceptions about young people. Today's students are often accused of having little regard for the quality of their work and for doing everything the fastest way possible.

To the contrary, I find when the importance of a project is elevated, students are willing and eager to improve their work. Elizabeth Haidle's beautiful book is certainly a prime example of such determination and enthusiasm.

The judges of the Written & Illustrated by... Contest were dazzled by the illustrations Elizabeth had prepared for the original book. All of the drawings were done with fine-line pen and colored pencils, and the delicacy of her illustrations and the softness of her colors were wonders to behold.

However, when Elizabeth arrived at our offices, she showed me some experimental water colors she had recently attempted and asked if I thought the illustrations for her finished book would be better if done in water color. I told her I admired her colored pencil renditions, but I thought water color would definitely be an improvement.

"I was afraid you'd say that," she grinned, "because it takes me five times as long to do them in water color."

Although I left the final decision to her, I had little doubt which medium she would choose. As you turn the pages of Elizabeth's lovely book, I'm confident you'll agree that her exceptional water-color illustrations are worth the effort.

The story of Elmer is not a simple one. It deals with individuality, behavioral problems, the loss of a pet, the death of a parent, loneliness, a special friendship, community spirit, and the reuniting of a family. Elizabeth wisely and skillfully tells her very touching story without allowing it to become overly sentimental.

Now enjoy this beautiful and sensitive book.

— David Melton
Creative Coordinator
Landmark Editions, Inc.

Deep in the lush green forests of Oregon, there are small mushroom villages that are inhabited by tiny beings called Elfkins. From dawn to dark Elfkins scurry about, gathering dewdrops, picking berries, and splitting twigs for firewood.

By nature Elfkins are cheerful, courteous and friendly, and they live together in peace and harmony. But once in a rare while, there is an exception. And this is the story about one such exception —
Elmer Ebaneezer Elwood the Third,
better known as Elmer the Grump.

The day Elmer the Grump had long awaited finally arrived — his eighteenth birthday. Elmer was now considered an adult who had the right to make his own decisions. And that's exactly what he intended to do. So, after eating his breakfast that morning, he marched to his room and packed his backpack.

"I'm leaving home for good!" Elmer announced. Then he picked up his tool chest and slammed the door behind him.

"Good-bye, Elmer," his mother and father called sadly.

But his eleven brothers and sisters shouted, "Good riddance!" because all of them agreed that Elmer was the grumpiest, grouchiest, crabbiest, crankiest, most disagreeable, ungrateful, ill-tempered, rude-mannered Elfkin they had ever seen.

Elmer didn't care what any of them thought. "I'm on my own at last," he said as he stomped down the road. "No more silly brothers and sisters to pester me! And no more bossy parents to tell me what to do!"

Because he didn't want his family to find him, Elmer walked for several days. One morning he saw a road sign pointing to Elfkinville. He quickly bypassed the village and went deeper into the countryside in search of the perfect place for his home. Before long he found it — a secluded meadow hemmed in by tall pine trees.

In the middle of the meadow grew a large mushroom that Elmer knew would make a fine house. Less than a stone's throw away was a smaller one, just right for a workshop. There was a bubbling spring nearby, and there were plenty of berries, nuts and wild herbs. Best of all, there were no houses in sight and no neighbors to bother him.

Eager to build his new home, Elmer walked to the big mushroom and quickly drew the outline of a door. Taking a hammer and chisel from his tool chest, he carved out a beautifully rounded doorway. Then he hollowed out space for three rooms and added a winding staircase. After he'd made a stove of scrap metal and built the furniture, his house was completed.

To keep out unwanted visitors, Elmer constructed a fence of prickly pine needles around his property. At the gate he hung a sign that warned: "NO TRESPASSING! BEWARE OF WILD BEES!" Elmer couldn't help but chuckle at that because he knew he didn't really have any wild bees.

In the tip of the smaller mushroom, Elmer hollowed out an attic where he planned to store acorns and wood. The first floor made a fine workshop, and there he built a sturdy oak worktable fit for a master woodcarver.

When it came to woodcarving, there was no doubt — Elmer was the best of the best. In his father's shop, he had learned to carve many things.

8

But Elmer decided to make just one product in his workshop — Christmas ornaments carved from acorns. It wasn't that the Grump really liked Christmas, but he knew other Elfkins did. He was sure he could make a lot of money selling his ornaments.

Since Elmer wanted no interruptions, not even from customers, he set up a mail-order business. He placed an advertisement for his ornaments in all the village newspapers, notified the Elfkinville post office of where he lived, and set a mail box outside his gate.

Elmer was now ready for business. He anxiously checked his mail box every morning, hoping to find orders. Finally two arrived, and he quickly ripped open the envelopes. The first customer wanted only one ornament, but the other Elfkin had ordered three!

"Well, it's not many orders, but at least I'm in business," Elmer reasoned. Before nightfall he had carved all four ornaments, packed them in boxes, and placed them in the mail box.

More orders arrived every day, and Elmer's business grew. This should have made him happy, but Elmer was such a grump that he never thought about being happy. The only thing that pleased him was to be left completely alone.

Every morning he worked in his shop, with no customers to interrupt him. Every afternoon he tended his garden, with no nosey neighbors to pester him. And at night, there were no snoring brothers or sisters to disturb him and no parents to tell him when to turn off the light. He could lie in his bed and listen to what he called, "the lovely silence."

One day Elmer was surprised to hear a knock at his front door.

"What do you mean by coming on my property?" he growled as he opened the door. "Can't you read the sign?"

"Good morning," the Elfkin lady said cheerfully, trying to ignore Elmer's rudeness. "My name is Elsa Louise, and I'm the headmistress of the Elfkinville Orphanage. We have twenty-four homeless children living there, and . . ."

"And I hope you keep those brats there!" Elmer retorted.

"I'll try," Elsa replied, "but it would be much easier to do if the orphanage were in better condition. The building needs a lot of repairs, and we need some help in fixing it up."

"I'm a woodcarver — not a carpenter."

"I understand," Elsa said politely, "but if you change your mind . . ."

"I never change my mind!" Elmer declared.

"Well, thank you for your time," she said, smiling again. Then she turned and walked away.

"How dare that woman smile like that!" Elmer fumed. "I should have used my 'wild bee' trick on her. Bet that would have wiped the smile off her face."

Since Elmer was so busy filling orders, autumn passed quickly for him. One morning the first chill of winter filled the air and snowflakes began to fall. Elmer knew he must hurry and gather another load of acorns. So he put on his coat and mittens and wrapped a warm scarf around his neck. Pulling his cart behind him, he faced the cold wind and made his way into the woods.

It was almost dark when Elmer loaded the last acorn on his cart and started home. Suddenly he heard a strange rattling sound. When he stopped and looked around, he saw a clump of leaves move. He picked up a stick and cautiously scattered the leaves. Then he saw what had made the noise — a little pink snail, shivering in the cold. Elmer leaned closer and saw that the snail was hurt. Her shell had a crack in it.

"You sure picked a cold day to get your shell cracked," he said bluntly, "but you're not my responsibility."

He turned to walk away. But when a gust of cold wind hit his face, Elmer knew he couldn't leave the little snail outside to freeze. He pushed the leaves aside, picked her up, and wrapped his scarf around her. Then he tucked the bundle inside his coat and hurried home.

As soon as Elmer entered his warm house, he placed the snail on the floor by the stove. She looked up at him and shivered again. Then she quietly rested her head on the floor.

Thinking the snail might be hungry, Elmer heated a bowl of beechnut broth and placed it before her. The little snail raised her head and sniffed, but didn't take a bite.

"Not good enough for you, huh?" Elmer scolded. "Then you can just go hungry, for all I care!" But when the snail laid her head back on the floor, Elmer realized she was too weak to eat. So he knelt down beside her and slowly spooned the broth into her mouth.

After the snail had eaten all she could, Elmer had to decide where she would sleep. She couldn't stay by the stove. The scarf might catch fire and burn down his house. He couldn't put her in the living room because she might leave slimy tracks on his chair. That left the bedroom.

Although Elmer didn't like the idea, he carried the snail upstairs and

12

placed her on the floor beside his bed. As he tucked his scarf securely around her, he warned, "Don't move from this spot!" Then he turned out the light and went to bed.

When the snail shivered and her shell rattled again, Elmer became even more annoyed. "Stop that shaking, or I'll throw you outside in the cold!" he threatened.

Although the little snail tried to hold still, she was so cold, she couldn't stop shaking and rattling.

"That does it!" Elmer growled, jumping out of bed. "I've got to do something with you, so I can get some sleep." But instead of putting the snail outside, he picked her up, placed her on the foot of his bed, and covered her with the corner of his blanket.

"And don't you dare snore!" he ordered, climbing back into bed. Soon both Elmer and the snail were fast asleep, and it was Elmer the Grump who snored the loudest.

13

Elmer was determined to get the snail out of his house as soon as possible, but first, he knew he had to help her get well. The next morning he fed her a special hazelnut porridge, and then he carefully examined the crack in her shell.

"This has to be cleaned, or it will become infected," Elmer said, taking a small bottle of dandelion alcohol from the cupboard. "Now, this is going to sting a little, but don't you dare cry!" he ordered.

The little snail pulled her head tightly into her shell. But she made no sound as Elmer poured a generous amount of the liquid into the crack and carefully removed the dirt with a milkweed fluff. Then he applied a bandage of eucalyptus leaves and secured it with thin strips of bark.

When he had finished, Elmer did an unusual thing, for a grump that is. He placed his hand on the snail's shell and gently patted her back. "Good girl," he told her.

Responding to his kind words and touch, the tiny snail raised her head and laid her antennae across Elmer's hand.

"Enough of that!" he bristled, trying not to look pleased. "I've got to get to work."

Not wanting to leave the snail in his house, Elmer carried her to his workshop. To make sure she wouldn't bother anything, he placed her at the back of his worktable where he could see her.

Between naps the snail watched Elmer's every move. Although the Grump wouldn't admit it, the snail's quiet attention pleased him. And in the late afternoon, when he noticed how the rays of the sun brightened

her delicate pink shell, he decided to name her, "Rosie."

And so their days together began. Morning and afternoon, Rosie accompanied Elmer to his workshop. In the evening after dinner, the two of them sat quietly in the living room. At bedtime Elmer carried Rosie upstairs to sleep . . . at the foot of his bed, of course.

The nourishing soups and herbal teas Elmer prepared helped Rosie to regain some of her strength. And every day he tended the crack in her shell and taped on a clean bandage. But the shell did not heal.

Grump that he was, Elmer complained about everything he did for the snail. If his grumblings bothered Rosie, she never showed it. And as the weeks passed, the Grump complained less and less.

One day, while Rosie slept on his worktable, Elmer couldn't help but notice the beautiful shape of her shell and the graceful lines of her neck. Taking a pencil from behind his ear, he drew Rosie's silhouette on an acorn. Then he carved the image of the little snail and polished the ornament to a glossy finish.

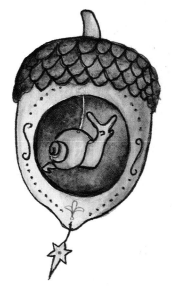

While Elmer worked, Rosie had awakened and crawled very quietly to the center of the table for a closer look. Now, everyone knows that snails don't smile. But as Elmer held up the finished ornament for Rosie to see, he was sure she had a smile on her face.

"No one will want to buy a Christmas ornament with a snail on it," Elmer said. "But if you like it, Rosie, we'll keep it." He placed it on the top shelf where it wouldn't get mixed in with the other ornaments.

15

But one morning, when Elmer took the ornament from the shelf to dust it, he made a startling discovery — THERE WAS NO SNAIL ON IT!

"No!" Elmer yelled. "It can't be!" He frantically checked every ornament in the shop, but the one with the snail on it was gone. "Some customer is going to think I'm stupid, and they'll never order from me again!" he stormed. "Rosie, did you see me mail out that ornament?"

Rosie just pulled her head deep inside her shell to wait until Elmer calmed down.

For the next several days, Elmer was grouchier and grumpier than ever. But toward the end of the week, he found a note that was attached to one of the new orders. When he read it, he was amazed.

> "Dear Sir: Yesterday I received my Christmas ornament,
> but it doesn't look like the drawing in your advertisement.
> Mine has a snail on it. Everyone loves this ornament, and I
> want to order ten more just like it!"

Soon Elmer's mailbox was packed with orders, and most of the customers wanted *snails* on their ornaments. Now Elmer really did have something to complain about. "I can't carve all these ornaments and get them shipped before Christmas!" he fussed. But by working late every evening, he finished all of the ornaments and got them in the mail.

Then on Christmas Eve, Elmer went into the woods and chopped off the tip of a young blue spruce. He stood the tiny tree in his living room and decorated it with spider's silk, holly berries, and beeswax candles of many colors. At the top of the tree he placed an ornament — one with a snail on it, of course. Rosie was so pleased.

For Christmas dinner Elmer roasted a huge walnut, seasoned with tasty herbs, and then he made a sparkling cranberry punch. To Rosie's surprise, there was a present beneath the tree. Elmer had carved a small acorn rocking chair, just for her.

After Christmas Elmer became more concerned about Rosie. The crack in her shell still had not healed, and with each passing day, she grew paler and weaker. But not wanting Rosie to know how worried he was, Elmer pretended to be cheerful. He prepared her favorite strawberry tea and kept her warm and moist. Sometimes he took her to the window so she could look outside. In the evenings he told her stories. And during the nights, Elmer often reached down to check Rosie's covers and make sure she was all right.

In spite of Elmer's fine care, one night Rosie became so weak she could no longer eat. Instead of going to bed, he sat in his chair, holding her in the curve of his arms.

The next morning, when Rosie did not respond to his touch, he knew his little friend had died. For some time he sat quietly, thinking how his life had changed since the day he found her shivering in the woods. Now he would be alone again.

Knowing what he must do, Elmer carried Rosie to the workshop and made a small wooden box. Tucking his scarf securely around the tiny snail, he gently placed her inside. Then, on a fine piece of wood, he carved Rosie's name and a garland of roses. Beneath her name, he carved her graceful form. As he polished the shell, he felt as if he were stroking Rosie's back.

Then Elmer walked to a small knoll a short distance from the house. He dug a tiny grave, lowered the box into it, and covered it over. After he placed the marker at the head of the grave, he stood there in silence for a long time.

During the months that followed, Elmer often turned from his work to look out the window at Rosie's grave. In the spring he planted flowers around the marker, and the site became more beautiful.

One morning in early summer, Elmer glanced up from his worktable and saw an Elfkin boy standing by Rosie's grave.

"WILD BEES! WILD BEES!" yelled the Grump as he ran outside and chased the boy away.

The following afternoon, the youngster returned. This time Elmer walked quietly to the knoll and surprised the boy.

"What are you doing here?" Elmer demanded.

"You won't call your wild bees, will you?" the boy asked.

"No," Elmer replied. "Just tell me why you keep coming here?"

"I come to look at this marker. Did you carve it?"

"Yes, I did," Elmer said rather proudly.

"I think it's beautiful," the boy exclaimed. "How much would you charge to carve such a marker for me?"

"More than you can afford," Elmer answered briskly, noticing the boy's worn clothing. "Besides, why do you want a marker?"

"It's for my mother," the boy explained. "She died three years ago and her grave still isn't marked."

"Why doesn't your father buy one?"

"I don't know where he is," the boy replied. "He left town years ago. I live at the orphanage."

"Well, I don't work for free," Elmer said bluntly.

The boy took a deep breath. "Sir, my name is Tyler," he said. "I notice your grass needs mowing and your garden needs to be weeded. If I work all summer for you, will you carve a marker for my mother's grave?"

Although Elmer didn't want anyone around, he knew he had many orders to fill and little time to do anything else. "All right," he agreed, "but I expect you to do a good job and never interrupt me while I'm working!"

20

"Yessir," the boy replied excitedly, handing Elmer a photograph. "My mother's name was 'Heather,' and you'll need her picture when you carve her face."

"Her face!" Elmer exclaimed. "I never agreed to do her face. I plan to carve only her name and a few flowers."

"But her face must be on it," Tyler insisted. "That's what makes Rosie's marker so special."

Elmer looked at the picture and then back at the boy. "You sure drive a hard bargain," he finally said. "Okay, I'll do it."

Tyler's face brightened with a smile, and he went right to work. Each morning he arrived early. Without interrupting Elmer, the boy mowed the grass and tended the garden. To Elmer's surprise, Tyler did even more than he had promised. He filled the water barrel, chopped firewood, and gathered acorns. Sometimes Elmer found a small present of sweet honeycomb outside the door.

Toward the end of summer, Elmer selected a fine piece of wood. As he had promised, he carved the marker. When it was finished, he called Tyler to come to the workshop. The boy rushed inside and looked at the marker for some time.

"It's very nice," Tyler finally said, "except there's something about my mother's face that isn't right."

"What do you mean, *not right?*" Elmer bellowed. "It looks exactly like the photograph."

"The face is the right shape," the boy explained, "but the eyes don't have the same warm look my mother's had."

" 'Warm look'? Nothing was said about carving *warmth!*" Elmer yelled, and he ordered Tyler out of his shop.

While Tyler worked that afternoon, he could hear Elmer storming about in the workshop. That evening Elmer was still so upset he couldn't eat.

And when he went to bed, he couldn't sleep.

"Warm eyes!" Elmer grumbled as he tossed and turned. "What a lot of nonsense!" But when the Grump pulled the covers up around his chin, he grew very quiet. He suddenly remembered how kind and loving his own mother's eyes were when she used to tuck him into bed. Then Elmer understood what the boy wanted. He jumped out of bed and rushed to his workshop.

When Tyler arrived the following morning, Elmer motioned for him to come inside. As the boy looked at the marker, the Grump asked nervously, "Well, what do you think?"

Tyler reached out and traced his mother's eyes with his finger. "The eyes are perfect now," he said quietly.

Elmer helped Tyler carry the marker to the village cemetery. Together they placed it at the head of the grave. As they stood and looked at the marker, the boy said, "Thank you," then raised his hand and slipped it inside Elmer's.

If Elmer felt uncomfortable with Tyler's gesture, he didn't complain.

By the time autumn arrived, Elmer was so busy filling orders, he didn't have time to gather enough acorns. He decided to find Tyler and ask him to work after school. Besides, he missed seeing the boy.

When Elmer went into the village that afternoon and saw the orphanage, he couldn't believe his eyes. The building was in worse condition than Elsa Louise had described. Elmer became so angry, he marched up the front steps and banged on the door. As Elsa opened the door, he blurted out, "This building is a disgrace! It's not safe for children!"

"That's what I tried to tell you and the Elfkins who live in the village," Elsa replied. "But no one would help us repair it."

"I'll help!" Elmer said, and even he was shocked that those words had come from *his* mouth.

"I can help too," said Tyler, running to the door.

"All the children will help," Elsa offered, "if you will teach them how."

Elmer was not at all happy about the idea of working with children. But he knew his own words had trapped him, and he decided to make the best of the situation.

That very day Elmer and Tyler found a fine place to build the new orphanage — a wide strip of land that had seven mushrooms growing in a circle. The largest mushroom was perfect for the main building. Six smaller mushrooms were just the right size for cottages for the children.

As soon as Elmer taught the children to use the tools, they began carving doorways and hollowing out the mushrooms. During the days that followed, everyone worked very hard, but the job was bigger than Elmer had thought. It was taking much longer than he had planned.

One morning the Grump was surprised when an Elfkin man rolled a wheelbarrow into the yard. "I came to help," the man announced.

"No thank you," Elmer said abruptly. "We can do it ourselves."

"Whatever you say," the man replied, "but if you want to get these buildings finished before winter, you'll need more help."

The Grump knew the man was right. Time was running out. The maple leaves had already turned red and were beginning to fall.

"We'll appreciate all the help you can give," Elmer finally agreed.

The man started working immediately. The next day three other Elfkins came to help. By the end of the week, most of the villagers had joined them. Sounds of building could be heard throughout the valley, and there was much joy and laughter as the community of Elfkins worked together.

24

When the last wall was painted and all the rooms were furnished, it was time to celebrate. Elfkins from miles around came to the party to eat their fill of almond crumb cake and to drink huckleberry punch. But while the others danced and sang, Elmer stood on the sidelines and watched.

"Why are you standing alone?" Elsa Louise asked him.

"I was just thinking how much I enjoyed working with everyone," he said. "My parents would certainly be surprised at that."

"Have you missed your parents?"

"I do now," Elmer admitted. "I even miss my brothers and sisters."

"Why don't you ask them to come for a visit?" she inquired. "Or do they live too far away?"

"They live in Elfkin Grove. It's not so far," Elmer said, "but I don't know if my family would want to see me again."

While Elmer had worked on the orphanage, hundreds of orders had piled up. He knew he would have to work day and night to fill all of them by Christmas.

Knowing Elmer needed help, Tyler packed ornaments every evening and on weekends. Other children from the orphanage helped, too, sweeping up wood chips and gathering acorns. They even brewed strawberry tea and made sandwiches. With so much help, all of the ornaments were finished and shipped in time.

On Christmas Eve Elmer sat alone in his comfortable chair. The house was very still, but the "lovely silence" was not so lovely anymore. Elmer couldn't help but think about Rosie. Then he thought about his parents. He wondered if they ever missed him as much as he missed them right now.

When Elmer awoke the next morning and opened the shutters, it was the most beautiful Christmas Day he had ever seen. The sun was shining brightly, and the freshly fallen snow glistened like tiny crystals scattered across the land. Elmer dressed in his best suit and strapped on his snow-shoes. Then picking up the present he had made for Elsa Louise and the children, he set out for the orphanage.

When the youngsters saw Elmer approaching, they called out, "Merry Christmas!" and urged him to hurry inside.

"I have a present for you," Elmer said cheerfully, handing the package to Elsa Louise.

Elsa removed the ribbon and opened the wrapping. "Oh, look what Elmer has carved for us!" she said excitedly, and she held up the ornament for all to see.

The children were delighted! "Thank you, Elmer!" they exclaimed as they gazed at their special gift. And when Elsa placed it at the top of the Christmas tree, the ornament seemed to glow with a shine of its very own.

"We have a surprise for you, too, Elmer!" Elsa smiled, and all of the children started to giggle.

"What could it be?" Elmer wondered.

Suddenly the kitchen door opened, and Elmer could hardly believe his eyes. There stood his mother, father, and his eleven brothers and sisters.

Hugs and kisses were warmly exchanged, and Elmer's parents told him they were so proud of him.

"Hooray for Elmer!" the children shouted and everyone joined in.

When the cheering stopped, Tyler walked over to Elmer. "I have something for you too," the boy said, and he held out a small willow basket.

"Open it! Open it!" everyone urged.

When Elmer removed the small cover from the basket, tears of joy filled his eyes. Nestled among the leaves was a tiny pink snail, with a name tag that read, "Rosebud."

"Thank you," Elmer said, rubbing his face with the back of his hand. "I think I have something in my eyes."

"Wow!" one of Elmer's brothers exclaimed. "Are you really Elmer the Grump who used to live at our house?"

"Not anymore," Elmer smiled as he picked up Rosebud and began to stroke her delicate shell.

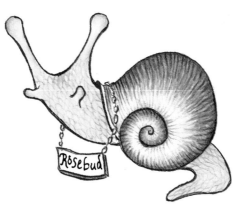

THE NATIONAL WRITTEN & ILLUSTRATED BY...

1988 WINNERS

Leslie Ann MacKeen

Elizabeth Haidle

Heidi Salter

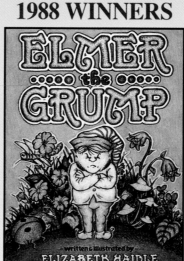

Who Can Fix It?
written and illustrated by
Leslie Ann MacKeen, age 9
winner of the 6-9 Age Category

As Jeremiah T. Fitz is driving to his mother's house, his car suddenly stops. "Who can fix it?" he asks. A bear, a kangaroo, a camel, and other animals offer suggestions that create hilarious situations. Leslie's narration is loaded with puns and humorous misunderstandings. Her stylized illustrations of Victorian settings are charming, and her colorful characters are very funny.

Hardcover   Library Binding
In Full Color   ISBN 0-933849-19-2

Elmer the Grump
written and illustrated by
Elizabeth Haidle, age 13
winner of the 10-13 Age Category

Elmer Ebaneezer Elwood the Third is the grumpiest, grouchiest, crankiest Elfkin anyone has ever seen. But once he helps an injured snail and befriends an orphan boy, Elmer learns to cherish the companionship of others.
Elizabeth's narrative offers a very touching story, and her beautiful illustrations add rich detail for readers to admire and enjoy.

Hardcover   Library Binding
In Full Color   ISBN: 0-933849-20-6

Taddy McFinley
and the Great Grey Grimly
written and illustrated by
Heidi Salter, age 19
winner of the 14-19 Age Category

Taddy McFinley's vivid imagination leads her to a confrontation with the monstrous Great Grey Grimly and on an exciting journey of mystery and suspense. With a clever sense of humor, Heidi's narrative offers high adventure, and her water-color illustrations explore the inner and outer realms of imagination and creativity.

Hardcover   Library Binding
In Full Color   ISBN: 0-933849-21-4

Landmark Gold Award Books

Before initiating The National Written & Illustrated by ... Awards Contest, Landmark published two students' books — WALKING IS WILD, WEIRD AND WACKY and THE DRAGON OF ORD. Both books were immediate hits with teachers and students.

Karen Kerber

David McAdoo

Walking is Wild & Wacky
written and illustrated by
Karen Kerber, age 12

A delightful picture book, filled with gentle humor and playful alliteration. Karen's brightly colored illustrations offer wiggly and waggly strokes of genius!

Hardcover
Printed in Full Color   ISBN: 0-933849-01-X

The Dragon of Ord
written and illustrated by **David McAdoo, 14**

An intergalactic adventure, hurling space ships into the future and forcing a final confrontation between the hero and the monstrous Dragon of Ord. David's skills as an illustrator are astounding!

Hardcover   Library Binding
Printed in Duotone   ISBN: 0-933849-23-0

Students' Published Books Entertain and Motivate!

Books for students, written and illustrated by students. What a wonderful idea! Thousands of schools nationwide have all of our students' books in their libraries, but the books are seldom on the shelves.

Students are fascinated with these books. The subjects are varied and popular, the illustrations are superb and eye-catching, and the reading levels are suited to the subjects. The students' books can stand on their own merit in full competition with books written and illustrated by adults.

Each book is an invitation and a challenge to the reader that he or she too can write and illustrate an original book. No better motivation can be found for inspiring students to write creatively or for encouraging them to read.

To obtain Contest Rules, send a self-addressed, stamped, business-size envelope to: THE NATIONAL WRITTEN & ILLUSTRATED BY ... AWARDS CONTEST FOR STUDENTS, Landmark Editions, Inc., P.O. Box 4469, Kansas City, MO 64127.

1987 WINNERS

Dennis Vollmer

Lisa Gross

Stacy Chbosky

Amy Hagstrom

Isaac Whitlatch

Dav Pilkey

Joshua Disobeys

written and illustrated by
Dennis Vollmer, age 6
winner of the 6-9 Age Category

Although Joshua's mother warns him not to go near the shore, the baby whale disobeys and becomes "beached."

Dennis skillfully tells of Joshua's misadventures and of the young boy who tries to help him. With a marvelous sense of design and an extraordinary display of overlaying colors, Dennis's amazing illustrations are absolute delights.

Hardcover   Library Binding
In Full Color   ISBN: 0-933849-12-5

The Half & Half Dog

written and illustrated by
Lisa Gross, age 12
winner of the 10-13 Age Category

One half of the half-and-half dog is Scottie, the other half is golden retriever. Because of his unusual appearance, he is laughed at and ridiculed. The half-and-half dog's search for acceptance and the discovery of his self-esteem is a touching and often hilarious story. Lisa's wonderful illustrations are colorful delights.

Hardcover   Library Binding
In Full Color   ISBN: 0-933849-13-3

Who Owns the Sun?

written and illustrated by
Stacy Chbosky, age 14
winner of the 14-19 Age Category

With full-color impressionistic illustrations and a flow of narrative that transforms prose into poetry, Stacy unleashes a powerful story and a plaintive cry for freedom. In her extraordinary book, she gently affects the mind and heart, as she touches an essential part of the human spirit and creates a meaningful experience for readers of all ages.

Hardcover   Library Binding
In Full Color   ISBN: 0-933849-14-1

1986 WINNERS

Strong and Free

written and illustrated by
Amy Hagstrom, age 9
winner of the 6-9 Age Category

When a herd of wild Appaloosas is threatened, a young boy and an old Indian try to save the ponies from capture. An exciting journey leads them to a lost canyon and to the unforgettable mystical vision of the Great White Stallion.

Amy's skillfully written narrative weaves an Indian legend into a modern adventure. Her lovely sponge-print illustrations are breathtakingly beautiful.

Hardcover   Library Binding
In Full Color   ISBN: 0-933849-15-X

Me and My Veggies

written and illustrated by
Isaac Whitlatch, age 11
winner of the 10-13 Age Category

The true confessions of a devout vegetable hater are told tongue-in-cheek by a boy who has met the enemy, spoonful by spoonful, and won. Isaac relates his madcap misadventures and offers readers surefire strategies for avoiding and disposing of the "slimy green things." His delightful color illustrations and his rib-tickling prose serve readers a finely chopped salad of laughter and mirth.

Hardcover   Library Binding
In Full Color   ISBN: 0-933849-16-8

World War Won

written and illustrated by
Dav Pilkey, age 19
winner of the 14-19 Age Category

When two kings, a fox and a raccoon, become embroiled in an arms race, each tries to build the tallest stockpile of weapons. When they realize their towers of powers could blow the world to smithereens, they work together in a search for peace. This timely parable, presented with humor and thought-provoking insight, offers hope for universal peace and understanding. It's a real winner!

Hardcover   Library Binding
In Full Color   ISBN: 0-933849-22-2

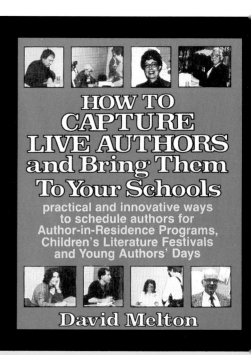